The Darcy

The Disappearance

MW01241059

The Darcys' First Christmas:
The Disappearance

Andrea J. Wenger writing as

Andrea David

The Darcys' First Christmas: The Disappearance

© 2016 Andrea J. Wenger

ISBN-13: 978-1541292703

ISBN-10: 1541292707

All Rights Reserved Worldwide

The author has asserted her rights to be identified as the author of this book. Duplication or distribution via any means is illegal and a violation of international copyright law, and subject to criminal prosecution. No portion of this literary work may be sold, manipulated, transmitted, copied, reproduced, or distributed, in any form or format, by any means or in any manner whatsoever, without the express written permission of the author, except for brief excerpts used for the purpose of review. To request written permission, contact Artesian Well Publishing at www.ArtWellPub.com.

All trademarks used herein are the property of their respective owners.

Published by

Artesian Well Publishing

www.ArtWellPub.com

Learn more about Andrea's books at AndreaDavidAuthor.com

This book is a work of fiction. All names, characters, locations, and incidents are the products of the author's imagination or are used fictitiously. Any resemblance to actual events, locales, organizations, or persons, living or dead, is entirely coincidental.

Published in the United States of America

Print edition, December 2016

Table of Contents

Chapter 1

Elizabeth Darcy descended the winding staircase in the London town house, her muslin day dress rustling against her petticoats. From each of the two necklaces draped across her hand, a gold cross hung. One was all simplicity, the other embellished with a diamond in the centre, and elegant flourishes at the tips.

Her temples ached with consternation as she strode into Darcy's study. He was leaning back in his chair, cravat loose, eyes scanning the newspaper. It still sometimes surprised her that this handsome man was her husband. His high cheekbones, his strong chin, his piercing dark eyes sent a flush through her.

Behind him, a fire crackled, light glinting against the polished green marble of the fireplace. The floors and bookcases were dark wood, but light poured in through the south-facing windows.

"What do you think, my love?" She approached the desk and showed him the necklaces. "I know Jane does not care about such things, but I am in a quandary. I would not wish to put on airs, but I do think the fancier necklace might be more fitting of my new station."

He rose and swept her into his arms. "This beautiful neck requires no adornment." He trailed kisses along her flesh, and a shiver ran over her.

She turned to kiss his mouth before saying, "That is lovely, but not helpful in my current predicament."

"You have never before shown much interest in jewellery. I suspect that you are driving yourself mad over a trifle because you are eager to see your sister."

Elizabeth's stomach fluttered. "I want everything to be perfect when Jane gets here."

"Because Jane is such a demanding critic."

Her shoulders fell, and she turned her head from him. He was right, of course. The sisters had not seen one another since their wedding day—a double wedding that all of Meryton and half of the surrounding county had turned out for—and she missed Jane dreadfully. She had so much to tell her, things one can only confide in a most beloved sister.

With a gentle fingertip, Darcy turned Elizabeth's face back towards his. "Jane will be so deliriously happy to see you, and you her, that you could both be naked and the other would not notice."

"I would not go that far."

"Perhaps I am arguing in favour of my wife being naked."

She looked at him slyly. "You *will* behave yourself once they get here, won't you?"

"Certainly. But I see no reason to do so before."

Darcy and Elizabeth had come to their London town house for the winter season immediately after their honeymoon tour of the Cotswolds. Elizabeth's only regret was that there had been no time to travel to her new home at Pemberley. She had not seen Darcy's beautiful estate since her trip to Derbyshire the previous summer, and she longed to learn all of its secrets.

She put on the necklace with the diamond, and Darcy clasped it for her. "I *do* need your help," she said, "to avoid any missteps. London is not Meryton."

"I seem to recall that at Netherfield last year, it was you schooling *me* on manners."

"The manners of a small town. Now it's time for you to return the favour."

"Surely you're not afraid of embarrassing yourself in front of Bingley and Jane?"

"No, but your uncle is an earl. I've never spent much time amongst the nobility."

"Elizabeth. You're a gentlewoman and my wife. You have nothing to fear."

She arched her brows. "I am not certain being your wife does much to endear me to the *women* of your acquaintance."

Hoof-beats drew Elizabeth's eyes to the window. A carriage came into sight. "Jane!" She rushed past her husband into the foyer.

"Some decorum, madam," he teased, and she gave him a backwards look.

Elizabeth wrapped a shawl around her shoulders and flung open the door. Jane was just stepping out of the carriage, a footman handing her down. Tendrils of blond hair escaped her bonnet and fluttered in the breeze. Elizabeth rushed down the brick stairs and into her sister's arms.

"Oh, Lizzy! How wonderful to see you. I have much to tell you. But first, let us get out of this chill before you catch your death."

The sisters rushed inside and gathered around the fire in the front parlour. Their husbands soon joined them. Servants took their coats and brought refreshments, while their carriage went ahead to take the Bingleys' bags to their own town house.

Once the visitors had warmed, they all sat and discussed the journey. "Do you know, Darcy," Bingley said, in the same jovial voice Elizabeth remembered, "that the old innkeeper at the Sheep and Hound is still alive and fit as ever? He served us the best leg of lamb I have ever had, did he not, Jane?"

"Oh yes, it was a rather humble place, but the food was quite good."

"Quite. And now, here we are in London. It's a fine place this time of year—I daresay we will have a merry time together."

"Lizzy, when did you say Georgiana will be joining us?" Jane asked.

"On Tuesday," Elizabeth replied. Darcy's sister, a young woman of seventeen, was arriving under the protection of Lady Adelaide, wife of Darcy's cousin, Viscount Astridge, heir to the Earl of Matlock.

"My mother has not stopped exhorting us to come to Longbourn for Christmas," Jane said. "She seems to expect it, no matter how often I explain we have other plans. I hate to disappoint her, but Bingley's family will all be here, and my brother Darcy's, too. If only my father could be convinced to come to London."

"It would do Mary and Kitty good to be in society here," Elizabeth agreed, speaking of their younger sisters. "And they would be so terrified, there would be no danger of them embarrassing themselves by doing anything *too* forward."

Jane shook her head. "You are hard on them, I think."

"Kitty is a pretty girl," Bingley said. "She is accustomed to being overlooked as one of five sisters. But with three of them now married, she has a chance to shine. And Mary...well, I imagine she has less time with her books now that Lydia is married. Your mother must require her company more."

Elizabeth nodded, surprised by the thought that Mary could improve by spending more time in their mother's company. Mrs. Bennet was a frivolous woman who cared mostly about clothes and gossip. But in fact, their mother's frivolity was the perfect antidote to balance Mary's quiet and studious nature.

"My sisters write," Elizabeth said, "that my father insists they spend a half-hour a day with him, Mary dancing and Kitty speaking French. He tells them they must find a husband if they want to have a roof over their heads once he is dead. Mary says, when that unfortunate event occurs, she'll come and live at Pemberley." Elizabeth gave her husband a sly look.

"We could build her a comfortable cottage all her own," Darcy replied.

"It's a pity women cannot go into the clergy," Elizabeth added. "She would be quite happy at the vicarage, marrying people and burying them and giving sermons on Sunday—like our cousin at Hunsford."

Jane covered her mouth with her hand, but too late to hide a smile. "Lizzy, you mustn't make me laugh at poor Mr. Collins."

"My apologies. He may be ridiculous, but he is quite earnest about it."

"You sound like my father, Lizzy," Jane said. "If you were not amongst friends, one might think you unkind."

"How thoughtless of me, dearest sister, to speak so unguardedly in front of your husband."

"Not at all," Bingley said. "Mr. Collins is a peculiar sort of man, but most respectable."

"Indeed he is." Darcy walked to the window and looked out. "Although it's extraordinary, the enthusiasm the reverend Mr. Collins shows for doing the minimum required of his position."

Elizabeth did not hide her pleasure at this observation. Even Jane fought a grin, and Bingley said in a happy voice, "Quite right!"

∽⊗∾

While the men enjoyed a brandy, the sisters went upstairs to the master bedroom and sat together on a grass-green divan in front of a window overlooking the garden.

"How was your trip to the Cotswolds?" Jane asked.

"My 'trip to the Cotswolds'?—is that what we're calling it?"

Jane gasped, pressing her hand to her chest. "Lizzy, do be serious."

Elizabeth eyed her sideways. "It was a most satisfying journey. The hills were magnificent—quite breath-taking, and larger than I expected."

Jane flushed a deep pink.

"I trust your journey also went well?" Elizabeth asked.

Jane bit her lip, then said at last, "It was a most pleasant excursion."

"Pleasant? Only pleasant?" she teased.

Jane rolled her eyes. "Very well, then. It was utterly blissful, and at times...a bit wild."

Elizabeth squealed, and Jane laughed and blushed.

"You must tell me everything," Elizabeth said.

"I shall tell you nothing." She sighed and grasped her sister's hands. "Dearest Lizzy, I am indeed the happiest of women!"

"I have no doubt, for you have the purest heart. But I must claim the title of second happiest."

"I am gratified to hear it. I have long wished for you to find a man who is your equal, and had despaired that such a one existed. But Darcy is your true match."

"He is. He tolerates my teasing with unfailing kindness. And he is quite the cleverest man I have ever known. But he does have his sombre moments. This time with Bingley will be good for him. I think he has missed him more than he says."

Jane smiled. "Poor Bingley says it enough for both of them. Not a day goes by that he does not lament, 'If only Darcy were here, he would have enjoyed that!' or 'That man is lucky Darcy is not here, he'd have quite put him in his place.'"

"Your husband is a most amiable man."

"He is! He never gets cross with me, Lizzy. He just turns quiet, so I know at once that he is vexed. We discuss it, and then...make up." Jane giggled, and Elizabeth joined her, squeezing her hands.

"Sometimes it seems quite wrong that I should be so happy," Jane said, "when others are not."

"Only you would think so, dear sister. You are happy because you were wise enough to make a suitable match."

"And fortunate to find one."

"I suppose I shall allow fortune to have some role. But you and Bingley deserve most of the credit."

"And you—mistress of Pemberley! How fine that is."

"I shan't feel like mistress of anything until we are settled in there. When I think back to my time there last summer, I do not know how I shall ever learn my way around."

"It is a most unfortunate problem to have," Jane teased.

"Indeed it is, having a home so grand I may get lost if I stray too far into the depths of it." Elizabeth smoothed her hair. "I know I am lucky. I only hope I prove deserving, and become a source of goodness to the neighbourhood."

"I have no doubt you will. You and Darcy will be known throughout the county for your generosity."

"Oh, Jane." A sudden pang in her breast brought tears to her eyes. "As gratifying as the prospect is, I do not know how I shall endure it with you so far away in Hertfordshire. Do you think Bingley might be prevailed upon to quit Netherfield, and let a house in the north?"

"I confess, the thought had crossed my mind. My mother seems to believe that Netherfield is as much her home as mine. She is forever there measuring for new drapes, or telling me we should order new plate. Bingley has only let the house for a twelve-month, and we're happy to make due until we decide where to settle."

"Derbyshire is quite beautiful, with the rolling hills and expansive vistas. My aunt Gardiner thinks it the most beautiful place in England, and I could easily be persuaded of it."

"Oh, Lizzy, I *have* missed you terribly. I shall talk to Bingley in earnest about it. You know how inclined he is to finding the good in everything, and overlooking the bad. But in truth, I think a house closer to you and Darcy, rather than one so close to Longbourn, would make us happier."

Warmth grew in Elizabeth's breast. Jane's absence had been the one enduring pain in the months since her marriage. Her stomach fluttered at the prospect of the Bingleys living within an easy distance of Pemberley.

On Tuesday, as expected, Miss Georgiana Darcy arrived in Lady Adelaide's carriage, a coach with four black horses. Lady Adelaide could not stay, but invited them all to tea the next day.

Jane and Bingley came to dine that afternoon, and Elizabeth could see the pains Georgiana took to make herself pleasing. Bingley she had known for some time, but she and Jane had only been in company once or twice before the wedding celebration.

Tall like her brother, with a light and graceful manner, Georgiana was a pretty girl and well-educated. She possessed all the accomplishments expected of ladies of her class, and indeed played the harp as well as Elizabeth had ever heard. Intelligent and well-informed, she nevertheless inclined towards a romantic nature that still required some governing at her tender age.

In the drawing room after dinner, Jane asked Georgiana, "How was your stay with your cousin's family?"

"Oh! most pleasant. Lady Adelaide was terribly kind to me, even though my cousin the viscount was in London on business much of the time. I worried that I would be a nuisance, but indeed felt perfectly at home there. The children are younger than me, none of them out yet. Lady Amelia will be presented at Saint James next year, and Lord Frederic expects to start at Cambridge the year after."

"They are nearer to your age than I expected, then," Jane said.

"Yes, and Amelia has such a lively nature, it is impossible to be unhappy in her company. If envy were not a sin, I should have fallen prey to wishing I had her ease."

"There are disadvantages to a lively nature as well, dear Georgiana." Elizabeth's heart ached at the girl's discomfort. "I have been accused more than once of speaking too freely."

A smile brightened Georgiana's eyes. "I have never heard anyone say so but my aunt, Lady Catherine de Bourgh, and she speaks more freely than anyone I know."

"Georgiana!" Elizabeth cried, but was too caught up in laughter to scold her.

A maidservant's knock interrupted them. "This express just arrived for you, ma'am."

Elizabeth's mood quickly shifted. An express? Her heart pounded. Urgent news could not be good. She rose and took the proffered envelope with trembling fingers, and the servant left with a curtsey.

"Whatever could it be?" Jane's voice was taut with anxiety.

"It is from Longbourn." Elizabeth choked on the words, panic gripping her throat as she ripped open the seal.

"You will excuse me," Georgiana said, stepping gently towards the door and closing it behind her as she left. As dear as Georgiana had become to her, Elizabeth was grateful for the girl's discretion. She would not wish Georgiana to see her initial reaction to the bad news—for bad it must surely be.

With Jane's arm linked in hers, Elizabeth read aloud the letter signed by her sister Mary:

Dear Eliza,

My mother has bid me write to say that Kitty has not been seen since yesterday evening. Her bed was slept in, so she must have left early this morning before the servants rose. My father is out looking for her, and my mother in great pains—with flutterings in her heart and constrictions in her chest, etc.—so it falls on me to write this letter.

Kitty's note said not to worry, for she had taken all necessary precautions for a safe journey, and we would all have a great laugh when we learned where she had gone. My mother, certain it is a kidnapping, is quite as distressed as when Lydia exposed our family to shame. Yet I have no fear of such a circumstance in this case. Kitty is not particularly clever, but she is more clever than that.

Your loving sister,

Mary Bennet

Jane paled and sank onto the couch. Elizabeth herself hardly knew what to make of it. Heaven knew what Kitty was capable of. Elizabeth paced, gathering her thoughts, trying to make sense of it and decide what must be done.

After a long silence, Jane said, "You do not suppose she might have eloped?"

"No, I must agree with Mary on that. Kitty is too ingenuous to disguise an assignation."

"But where on earth could she have gone?"

"She *has* been unhappy—my father has been stricter with her than usual. But requiring her to do one sensible thing a day cannot be such a hardship that she would abandon her home. She may have lost Lydia's company, but she has Maria Lucas. She is not utterly friendless."

"I cannot make sense of it, Lizzy!"

"That's because it is not a sensible thing. No, we must think in other terms altogether."

Jane drew her brow. "You and I may regard her as a child, but indeed she is not. She is a grown woman now. Perhaps she wants to make her own decisions."

"But Jane, do not her actions show how little prepared she is to be trusted on her own? Sneaking out like a thief, with nothing but a note to assuage my parents' worry?"

"What shall we do, Lizzy? How may we be of use?" Jane drew her brow. "I suppose we must go to Longbourn."

"I suppose we must. My mother will get her wish after all, of having her family around her at Longbourn for Christmas..." Elizabeth halted, turning over the idea in her mind.

Jane sat forward. "You do not think—"

"No, I don't. At least, not that my mother could have put her up to it."

"What a wicked thought! And yet...No, I shall not think it. Kitty must have had some other intention, a friend in need, perhaps."

"What friend? Apart from her sisters and aunt and uncle, she barely knows a soul outside of Meryton."

"Kitty has led such a sheltered life—she would not have simply run away? She must be running towards something, or someone."

A knock came on the door, Darcy's knock. Elizabeth recognised it at once. "Is everything well, my love?" his muffled voice asked.

She opened the door and sank into his gentle embrace. "I cannot yet say, for we have had the most puzzling news. Kitty has left Longbourn for heaven knows where, and of course, my parents are assuming the worst."

They made their way back inside the drawing room, Bingley on their heels. Georgiana hovered in the hallway. Elizabeth motioned for her to join them, then closed the door so the servants would not overhear.

"We must keep our wits about us," Elizabeth said. "Assuming that no harm has come to her—and there's no reason to think it has, given her note—then there are only a few places she could have gone. To Jane or me, to my aunt and uncle Gardiner, or to—"

"Lydia," Jane finished. "Goodness, could it be?"

"Lydia is the only person Kitty has ever been able to keep a secret with," Elizabeth said.

"Kitty *has* been pestering my father to let her visit Lydia, but he refuses."

"For obvious reasons," Elizabeth added.

"Oh dear," Jane said, "I think that must be the answer."

"Well, then," Bingley said, "that's the end of it. We call on Lydia—"

"Easier said than done." Elizabeth brushed a tendril of dark hair back from her forehead. "Lydia likes to give the impression that she and Wickham are staying somewhere stylish, but she won't give an address. She's come by here a couple of times since we got to London, but she won't let me return the visit."

"I shall find them," Darcy said, resignation in his voice.

Elizabeth gave him a fond smile. "It is becoming rather an annual event for you."

As soon as the words left her lips, she regretted them. She turned to see Georgiana with her eyes down and a deep blush on her cheeks.

"Oh, Georgiana!" She went and sat next to the girl, squeezing her hand. "That was thoughtless of me."

Tears came to Georgiana's eyes. The girl rose and said, "I beg your pardon," as she quickly walked out.

"Darcy," Elizabeth said, "I am so sorry. How stupid of me."

"I shall go after her."

Elizabeth watched him leave, a heaviness in her heart. The reminder of Georgiana's own near-elopement with Wickham two years prior could only cause the girl pain. And for Elizabeth to make light of it—how callous she must seem! Could Georgiana forgive her? And could Darcy?

Surely Lady Catherine was no longer the only member of the family who thought Elizabeth spoke too freely.

Chapter 2

Elizabeth discussed Kitty's situation with the Bingleys for a while longer. The three concluded that in all likelihood, Kitty had travelled to London—so there was not much use in their all going to Longbourn, at least not until they received more information. Elizabeth sent her parents a message to that effect, adding that she and Jane were at their command, while Darcy and Bingley would try to root Kitty out using their contacts in town.

Darcy and Bingley left shortly before nightfall to see what they could learn. Elizabeth and Jane stayed in the drawing room, making a list of their sisters' acquaintances. They remained convinced that London was Kitty's only reasonable destination.

Georgiana did not come when called to supper, so a tray was sent to her room. Elizabeth had never in her life felt more guilty at speaking a careless word.

"Do not torture yourself so," Jane said. "You did not intend any harm."

"Yet I have done it nonetheless. Georgiana is a sweet girl. To remind her of such a painful chapter in her life is unforgivable. The thought of it fills her with such shame—it is evident every time Wickham's name is spoken. And for me to tease Darcy about it in her presence...it was foolish of me indeed."

"But what she did was not so very bad. She confessed her plans to Darcy. And even if she had gone so far as to elope with Wickham, there can be no doubt that he truly intended to marry her."

"No doubt at all. He had thirty thousand reasons to marry Georgiana. Lydia's enticements were far less." If Darcy had not paid Wickham to marry Lydia, she would have been ruined.

"Our family is very much in Darcy's debt," Jane said. "And we will likely find ourselves indebted to him again, for locating Kitty."

"What could that girl have been thinking?"

"Lydia must be terribly lonely," Jane observed. "It does not surprise me that she should long to have Kitty by her side, especially at Christmas. If Wickham is too unwell to travel—"

"Whether Wickham is unwell, or merely wishes to avoid the company of his family at Longbourn, has not been established to my satisfaction. He ventured all the way to London from the north to recuperate from his injury. Surely he had friends enough left in Derbyshire that he might have found a place there, if his injury truly made travel such a burden."

"You think he had some other reason for coming to London?"

"None in particular. But there are far more entertainments for a dissolute man in London than in Derbyshire."

"Poor Lydia. I hope marriage has improved his tendencies."

Elizabeth chuckled. "One can always hope."

"Indeed, his circumstances now are likely better than they ever have been before. He has his officer's pay in addition to whatever Darcy settled on him for Lydia. The two of them ought to be able to live quite comfortably."

"You and I could live quite comfortably on an officer's pay. What does Lydia know of economising? If there are coins in her reticule, she must spend them. The sound of them jangling together would drive her into a nervous fit otherwise."

Jane nodded. "That is not her fault."

"Heavens, no. She was not taught any better. Still, if she had stayed at home a few more years, rather than eloping with the first man who paid her more than a passing notice, she might have had time to learn." Elizabeth leant back and stared at the ceiling. "What if we are wrong? What if Kitty *has* eloped?"

"I cannot picture it. Mary is right about one thing. Kitty is too clever to think it a good idea."

"And she is not clever enough to manage it. If she were that desperately in love, she would not be able to keep it to herself."

Jane pursed her lips. "She has barely said a word about any man in particular since the officers left Meryton, and that has been six months. No, I simply do not believe an elopement is possible."

Noise in the hallway announced the gentlemen's return. Unfortunately, they had discovered nothing substantial, but at least, as Darcy put it, they had uncovered some of the places where Kitty was *not*. Jane and her husband went home shortly after, Bingley promising to re-join Darcy in the search the next morning.

Alone with her husband, Elizabeth felt a tight knot of dread in her stomach. "I am sorry to put you through so much trouble," she said as they dressed for bed.

"Do not apologise. You are not at fault."

"It seems my family has caused you nothing but trouble. You must be wondering whatever possessed you to marry me."

He came to her in his shirtsleeves and set his hands upon her waist. "I am thinking nothing of the kind. On the contrary, I am wondering what I might have done differently when Wickham and I were at Cambridge, before he was so set in this life of dissolution, to have spared your family the pain of this connection. If anyone in the world could have set Wickham on a different path, it is I."

"Surely you cannot blame yourself!"

"I made a few small attempts at the time to break him of his bad habits—but when they failed, I cut ties with him. I believed it was my duty, but in fact, the loss of my influence and my friendship may only have set him on an even worse path than he might otherwise have taken."

"Yet to remain friends with such a man would have put your own reputation at risk—and your family's."

"Some young men are wild in their university years and grow into respectable gentlemen. Wickham might have been the same if I had not abandoned him to the influence of his profligate friends. So you must not rebuke yourself, my dear. You have not thrust Wickham on me. I have thrust him on you. And I am prepared to do everything in my power to mitigate the harm he causes the innocent."

"I am not certain Kitty may be called innocent. She is not a child—she is nineteen. She knows better than to cause this worry to her family."

"My dear," he said, taking her hands, "I hope you will not mind my sharing an observation. As Bingley pointed out last week, Kitty is accustomed to being overlooked. When I was staying at Netherfield, it seemed your father never spoke of Kitty except to observe how silly his three youngest daughters were. And your mother favoured Lydia over her to such a degree that it was painful to watch. Even my cold heart was moved by it."

"You do not have a cold heart."

"Certain observers seemed to think so."

"You mean they mistook you for someone who does not feel strong emotion, simply because you do not show it—just as you mistook Jane?"

"I deserved that. But indeed, if Kitty is accustomed to going unnoticed, one can hardly be surprised if she assumed her disappearance from Longbourn would be of no great inconvenience. Her father would not permit her to see her sister, so she went without his permission. One might even regard that as a logical progression."

"Only for one as ungoverned as my younger sisters have been."

"It is not Kitty's fault that she has been ungoverned. It can be of no surprise that she has rebelled against your father's sudden interest in her education, when neither of her parents paid any mind to it for the first eighteen years of her life."

"You are very philosophical about this."

"I have had two years' practice, convincing myself that Georgiana's plan to elope with Wickham did not reflect a failing in her character but in her education. Georgiana has always been an obedient, thoughtful girl, but I was quite deceived in placing her with Mrs. Younge. So might Kitty prove to be a young woman of fine character under the right influence."

Elizabeth sat on the edge of the bed, deep in thought. "We should invite her to Pemberley."

"We should. You do not wish it?"

"I love Kitty of course. She will be a handful."

"Perhaps not, in a different environment. With Georgiana as a role model, rather than Lydia, she might do quite well."

"One can only hope." Elizabeth shook her head. "I hurt Georgiana terribly tonight. She will not even speak to me."

"I think you are mistaking her shame for resentment. I am the resentful one in the family, remember? I believe Georgiana reflects bitterly on the fact that she allowed herself to be flattered and deceived by Wickham. Perhaps she doubts your affection for her, because she was so deceived in his."

"What can I do?"

He kissed her. "Sleep. Things will look better in the morning."

She ran her fingers down his chest. "You are not angry with me?"

"On the contrary, I am furious with you. But you are just as angry at yourself, and no unkindness was meant. The fact remains, Georgiana nearly threw her life away on the most worthless man of her acquaintance. It pains her to be reminded of it, but it was her own choice. She must learn to respond in a more ladylike fashion than locking herself in her room the next time the subject comes up. And it *will* come up. Lydia will come to Pemberley from time to time, and Georgiana will be faced with what her life might have been."

"Lydia. At Pemberley? I did not think you would permit such a thing."

"*He* will not be permitted. *She* may visit her sister on occasion." Darcy took Elizabeth's hands. "I shall never forget the look on your face that day in Lambton, when you received the letters about Lydia's elopement. You could not have been so distraught if you had not felt a deep and inalienable love for your sister. Whatever Lydia may have done, and whatever she may do in the future, she will always be one of the dearest people in the world to you, and I would never interfere with that."

Tears streamed down Elizabeth's face, the terror of those hours in Lambton still fresh in her heart.

Should she not fear just as much for Kitty? No; for Kitty was not in the power of a treacherous man like Wickham. Kitty knew what was required for a lady to travel under respectable circumstances, and would not embarrass her family. Elizabeth had faith that Kitty would be well—she had had no reason to think the same of Lydia.

And if not for Darcy, Lydia might indeed have been ruined. Her family owed him so much, and now they were in his debt again.

"I am amazed that I have found the great good fortune to have married a man with so much true goodness as you."

"Come now, Lizzy. Remember how I was when you first met me. Arrogant, above all my company, and steadfastly refusing to be charmed by you."

"Indeed, that is unpardonable."

He kissed her deeply. "Have I told you how grateful I am that you refused my first proposal? I would still be that same insufferable man if you had accepted me. And I might have had moments when I wondered if you had married me solely to raise your family's circumstances. Now I know that the only thing that could have induced you to marry me was love."

"Seeing how angry my mother was at my refusing Mr. Collins' proposal, I can only imagine her fury if she had known I had refused you." She shook her head. "Truly, if Wickham's lies had not convinced me of your bad character, I might have been tempted by your offer. We might both of us be as foolish now as we were then. So indeed, we are indebted to Wickham for his duplicity."

"It still pains me to hear the man's name."

"Me as well. But as you say, he is part of our lives, and we must get used to it."

⁂

Elizabeth woke with a start at dawn, the previous day's worries flooding back. Darcy tried to soothe her, but it was of no use. Not only did Kitty's disappearance weigh on her, but the rift between herself and Georgiana pricked at her heart.

She dressed and headed downstairs, hoping to speak with Georgiana as soon as the girl descended.

Darcy left soon after to begin the quest from the night before anew. Once he was gone, the house remained quiet for two more hours, with no one about but the servants. She rattled through the empty rooms alone, desperate for news from Longbourn.

What had her father learned? If Kitty had taken a companion with her—which surely she would have, since a lady never travelled alone—someone in the neighbourhood would have known. Perhaps that would give them a hint of where Kitty had gone, and help them track her steps.

"Oh, Kitty, how could you be so irresponsible?" Elizabeth said to the air.

At last, the sound of slippered feet on the staircase drew Elizabeth into the foyer. Georgiana looked pale in a white muslin day dress with a yellow sash at the waist.

"Sister, I am so glad to see you up. I began to fear you were unwell. Cook has made you your favourite breakfast—"

"I am quite well, Elizabeth, no need to fuss over me."

"But I am not well. I am not well at all." Tears sprang to her eyes. "My heart is broken, dear Georgiana, to know that my careless words injured you. Can you forgive me? I understand if you are angry—"

"Dear Elizabeth!" Georgiana wrapped her arms around her. "I could never be angry at you. I am so ashamed of myself. It is my fault your sister is missing. If I had not been so deceived in Wickham—"

"I daresay you were not the first unfortunate woman to be deceived in Wickham, and you were surely not the last." Elizabeth drew Georgiana into a tight hug, relief flooding through her. Her duty to be a good sister to Georgiana ranked just below her duty to be a good wife to her husband. Moreover, Georgiana was an easy girl to love, so shy and self-deprecating. Elizabeth wanted to be not just a good sister but a good friend.

"I had fancied myself to be an astute judge of character," Elizabeth continued, admiring the little flush of colour that had risen in Georgiana's cheeks, "until your brother revealed to me how utterly mistaken I had been about Wickham, and about himself. A year ago, I believed Wickham to be the pleasantest man of my acquaintance. I was as convinced of his charms as anyone has been. Indeed, the entire village of Meryton was deceived in the man. The fault is in him, not in you, dearest Georgiana. I do not want you to have another moment's unease on that account. Promise me you will not blame yourself for his failings. Promise me."

"I promise." Georgiana gave her a smile, which Elizabeth was happy to return.

As soon as they had breakfasted, a knock came at the door. Elizabeth's heart fluttered with hope of another express from Longbourn. Instead, her aunt Gardiner had come to see if they had any news.

Elizabeth was never disappointed to see Mrs. Gardiner, a woman of sense and breeding. Her husband, Elizabeth's uncle, was in trade in town and a credit to the family. Still, Elizabeth could not help but feel a pang in wishing to know if her father had found out anything about Kitty's whereabouts.

They sat in the music room, and Georgiana played her harp. The music soothed the turmoil in Elizabeth's head, if only for a short while.

The housekeeper brought in a tray of tea and biscuits. "Begging your pardon, ma'am, but a pot of mint tea always revives my spirits. I thought you might enjoy it."

"Yes, Davis, that is very kind."

Once Davis had gone, Mrs. Gardiner said, "I do not think the situation is quite as serious as it might appear at first glance. A grown woman may visit her sister without any impropriety at all. While I cannot approve of her method, I can understand that she might have become desperate after her father's repeated refusals. She and Lydia were constant companions from the day Lydia was born. Surely this separation has been dreadful for her. Although one cannot fault your father. If he were to let Kitty visit Lydia, it would have to be in the company of you or I or Jane."

"You are right as always, Aunt."

"What do you think, Lizzy? Would it be objectionable, once this is over, to invite Kitty to stay with Mr. Gardiner and me for the winter, without inviting Mary? As much as I would wish to have dear Mary with us, too, I could not deprive your mother of *all* her daughters."

In her mind, Elizabeth could not help congratulating Mrs. Gardiner; for Mary's company could be tedious, and finding a benevolent reason for excluding Mary from the invitation was a clever trick. And her aunt was quite right—her mother would be unable to endure losing the companionship of *all* of her daughters; and for Mary's part, she was no more likely to be drawn from her books by the diversions of town than those of the country. "I think that is a fine plan. Kitty would be most grateful, I am sure."

Another knock came at the front door, and this time, Elizabeth did not dare get her hopes up. But as luck would have it, a minute later, Davis brought them the much-awaited letter from Longbourn, this time from her father.

Dearest Lizzy,

It would seem that you and Jane were right to stay in London, as I am convinced your foolish sister Kitty has indeed travelled there.

I knew her to have a particular friendship with the daughter of one of tenant families, a Miss Smithson, who apparently does fine needlework that all the ladies admire. Well, I asked old Smithson about his daughter, and he claimed no knowledge of where she had gone. The man's young son piped up, "But we do, sir, she has gone to town with Miss Bennet, and David, too!"

Perhaps old Smithson thought I would be cross that his son and daughter had helped Kitty make her escape, but of course they would not have known she had left without permission. I thanked the old man, and gave the boy tuppence for his trouble.

I was able to ascertain that they left at eight in the morning on the express to London. I spoke to the driver this morning, and he confirmed taking a lady and two servants as far as _____ Street yesterday. Perhaps Darcy or Bingley could trace her from there.

Your loving father, etc.

"Why, this is wonderful news!" Mrs. Gardiner said. "She is travelling with a maidservant and a manservant, as she ought to be. And she is in London, perhaps just a few blocks away. All will be well, I am sure of it."

"Indeed, we must let Jane know at once."

"Oh, yes, I shall go with you to tell Jane the news. She will be so relieved."

"Georgiana, would you like to come?"

A bright smile broke across the girl's face. "I would be happy to see Mrs. Bingley. She is such a kind and gentle person."

The three ladies made their way to the Bingley's town house. Elizabeth gave her sister their father's letter, and Jane was much comforted by it.

"Is Miss Bingley at home?" Elizabeth asked regarding Mr. Bingley's sister Caroline, who lived with him.

"She and her sister went to a musical performance. I was supposed to go with them, but I dared not in case some word came about Kitty."

"So they left you here alone?"

"It is fine, Lizzy. Sometimes one would rather keep one's own company."

"Miss Bingley is a fine lady, is she not?" Georgiana asked.

"Yes, she is," Elizabeth said diplomatically, "and she has a very high opinion of you. When she was at Netherfield, I do not believe I had a single conversation with her where she did not sing your praises."

"Why, I cannot imagine what I might have done to win her approbation, but I am grateful for it."

"You are an accomplished young woman, and Miss Bingley reveres accomplishment."

"Oh!" Georgiana's face fell.

Flustered once again by the girl's ingenuous nature, Elizabeth took her hands. "My dear Georgiana, you must learn that while I may tease everyone else you know, I shall never tease you, for you have no faults worth making fun of. You're a sweet, intelligent girl and a most devoted sister. You are like Jane in that your only fault is your reluctance to see the faults in others."

A bright smile adorned Georgiana's face. "To be compared to Mrs. Bingley is a great compliment indeed."

A frantic knock came at the door. Elizabeth jumped to her feet, heart beating wildly.

Jane did not wait for the housekeeper. Rushing into the foyer, she looked out the sidelight and gasped.

When she flung the door open, Kitty fell into her sister's waiting arms. "Oh Jane!" Kitty cried. "Wickham is the most horrid man on earth."

Chapter 3

Elizabeth's heart pounded and her thoughts flew. Relieved as she was to see Kitty, terror froze her blood at her sister's words. Every unthinkable thing became thinkable in that moment. If Wickham had harmed...if he had violated Kitty, Elizabeth would not rest until justice was done.

"What happened?" Jane asked, leading her to the fire. She looked to their aunt.

"Come, Georgiana," Mrs. Gardiner said. "Have you seen Jane's piano? I long to hear you play, after the way your brother praises you." She led the girl out and closed the door.

"Kitty, you must tell us everything," Elizabeth said. "Do not hold back. We are your sisters, and we will ensure that you are protected."

"I know my father must be furious with me," Kitty said, apparently confused about whom Elizabeth thought she needed protection from. "When Wickham refused to come to Longbourn for Christmas, Lydia came up with the perfect scheme. I would run away to London to join them, and then Wickham would have to return me home. It would be the only gentlemanly thing for him to do."

Elizabeth might have laughed aloud at that remark if not for the horror still lurking in her breast.

Kitty stomped her foot. "But Wickham steadfastly refused. He grumbled last night that there was nowhere for me to sleep, and barely food in the cupboard to feed me. Lydia made him sleep on the floor so I could have the bed with her. Which did not put him in a better mood this morning, I assure you."

Elizabeth cupped Kitty's face in her hands. "But Wickham did not harm you?"

"He was abominable to me!"

"But he did not...touch you?"

"No, why on earth would he touch me?"

Elizabeth let out a long breath and held Kitty tight. "Do you have any idea how worried we have been, and my parents, too?"

"It was not supposed to be that way. We were supposed to leave for Longbourn right away, or this morning at the latest. Lydia had it worked out, but it did not go that way at all. And then this morning, when Wickham got that letter—"

"Well this is a fine thing," Bingley said as he entered through the front door, Darcy behind him. "We spend the morning traipsing across the city, then stop in at Darcy's for some dinner, only to find..." He broke off, eyes landing on Kitty. "My dear sister!" He rushed forward and kissed her cheek. "You have sent us on a fine goose-chase. I could not be happier to see you."

"I am relieved you are well, Kitty," Darcy said in a gruff tone.

"I am sorry to have put you out. It is all Wickham's fault."

"Kitty, it is not Wickham's fault!" With Elizabeth's fear gone, so was her patience. "Lydia came up with a ridiculous scheme, you went along with it, and Wickham did not. It is entirely your fault."

"If Wickham were any kind of gentleman—"

"Wickham is no kind of gentleman," Elizabeth said in a stern voice. "A gentleman does not seduce a sixteen-year-old girl with no intention of marrying her."

"But he *did* marry her!"

"Because Darcy paid him to."

"Elizabeth," her husband objected.

"No, she needs to hear this. She needs to understand what a dissolute man our brother Wickham truly is. You once said, Darcy, that you blamed yourself for the fact Wickham was accepted into Meryton society. That if your pride had not stopped you from exposing the man, that Lydia might have been spared. It is time for Kitty to know the truth so that *Kitty* may be spared."

Elizabeth turned to her sister. "Wickham is a liar, a seducer, and a thief who buys on credit and leaves town without paying his debts. You are not safe alone in his company. He is a military man trained to kill. He is capable of doing you violence, Kitty. Do not underestimate him, or it could cost you dearly."

The room fell silent as tears streamed down Kitty's face. She sank onto the couch. "Is he really that bad?" she asked in a small voice. "Lydia's husband?"

Jane sat beside her. "We have no proof that Wickham is a violent man, only the fear of it. You mustn't fret for Lydia's sake. But you cannot trust him to do right by you. He has never done right by anyone—least of all himself."

Darcy took Elizabeth into his arms. She trembled violently, but his touch soothed her. "I have known Wickham his whole life, and I do not believe he would harm Lydia bodily. He is not so bad as that. But you cannot trust a word he says to you, Kitty. It pains me to say it, but it is true. I loved him like a brother once, but he is forever lost to me. I would advise you to treat him as your older sisters do. They are civil, but always on their guard. You must assume every word that comes out of his mouth is a lie."

"But he is the kindest, friendliest man!"

"Friendly, but not kind," Jane said. "That is all appearance, I am afraid."

"Kitty," Bingley said, "this is hard for you to hear, I know. Your sisters are concerned for your well-being. They did not tell you this before now, because they wanted to protect you from the truth. Now it's clear that knowing the truth is the only way to protect you. You're a good girl, Kitty. I understand how close you and Lydia are. But it's time for you to look to your older sisters rather than to your younger one. Following *their* example will lead you on a path to a happy life."

Jane rose. "I must write to my father, and let him know you are here."

"I shall call my man to take the letter right away," Bingley said.

The Bingleys exited, and the Darcys sat on either side of Kitty. Elizabeth took her hand. "You said Wickham got a letter this morning?"

"Yes, he is expected to re-join his regiment in the north after the new year. The military surgeon who examined him said he should have made a full recovery by then."

"And he objects?" Elizabeth asked.

"Mainly, he objects that his request for a transfer was denied. He is being sent back to the same regiment, even though Colonel Fitzwilliam tried to kill him."

Elizabeth's breath stopped.

"He what?" Darcy demanded.

"Wickham said that Colonel Fitzwilliam put him in the most dangerous position during the training exercises, and that's why he was injured."

"Colonel Fitzwilliam says Wickham was injured because he was drunk on duty."

"Neither of those things excludes the other," Elizabeth observed. "They might both be true."

"Half a dozen men can confirm that Wickham was drinking until the small hours of the morning the night before. A commanding officer less generous than my cousin might have put Wickham before a court-martial. Instead, he received only a reprimand." Darcy rose and shook his head, walking to the window. "The man could have lost his leg. He was lucky no one else was injured."

Elizabeth rose and laid her hand on her husband's arm. "Surely you do not believe anyone would take Wickham's word over that of an honourable man like Colonel Fitzwilliam?"

"Why not? You took Wickham's word for it when he painted me as a blackguard. The man is capable of ingratiating himself with anyone."

Elizabeth swallowed and pursed her lips. "That is true."

"Is Wickham really *so* bad?" Kitty asked.

"He seduced your sister," Elizabeth said. "What more evidence do you need?"

Kitty fidgeted. "Do you think everyone was deceived in him? Even his friend Denny?"

"All of Meryton fell under the man's spell. I don't see why Denny would be—" Elizabeth stared at her sister. "Why are you asking about Mr. Denny?"

Kitty looked away.

The turmoil in Elizabeth's breast, so lately relieved, quickly rose again. "Tell me you are not corresponding with him!"

"No, of course not, that would be improper."

Elizabeth was not so easily put off. "Kitty, what are you not saying?"

"My aunt Philips is corresponding with him. She lets me see his letters. Sometimes she allows me to add a line or two to hers."

Elizabeth sank onto the couch next to her sister. "Does my father know about this?"

"I am not doing anything wrong!"

"No, you are merely carrying on a love affair, with my aunt Philips as the intercessor!" Mrs. Philips was her mother's sister, and equally as frivolous.

"It is not a love affair. Lydia was always Denny's favourite. He feels quite ill-used by Wickham, but he has no interest in me."

Elizabeth took Kitty's hands. "It will do you no good to pine away for him, just because he's the first man you ever liked. What would you say to wintering in town with my aunt Gardiner, if my parents approve?"

"Might I? Oh, Lizzy, that would be splendid!"

"If you wish for my father's permission, then you must be very contrite, and acknowledge your fault in this scheme. You must not blame Lydia or Wickham. Oh, and you must be kind to my uncle Gardiner, too, for my aunt and I only devised the plan this morning, and he has not heard a word of it. It would make a good start if you were to find my aunt, and tell her how very sorry you are for distressing her."

"I shall." The sisters rose. "Oh, Lizzy!" Kitty hugged her before exiting to the drawing room, from which could be heard a Mozart sonata.

Elizabeth looked over at Darcy wearily. "Our children will have two governesses each, to watch their every move until their wedding day. And perhaps after."

"Our children will run and jump and play in Pemberley Woods until they exhaust themselves, and know all the delicious freedoms of childhood. But they will also be instructed in music and literature and philosophy, and have the foundation for a moral life." He took her in his arms and kissed her temple.

"Well," he said, "it appears that this has turned out better than could be expected."

"Has it?" she asked. "I cannot help wondering whether there's more to Lydia's side of the story."

Jane sent the missive to Longbourn and requested instruction from their father as to how to deliver Kitty home. She was welcome to stay with the Bingleys for Christmas, Jane wrote, and indeed, all the sisters welcomed the idea. It was apparent to the older two that the atmosphere at Longbourn was not conducive to the development of Kitty's character. For Kitty herself, it was unbearable.

Those closest to Kitty were perhaps unable to see her worth. Where her own father described her as foolish or silly, Bingley called her a good girl, a pretty girl. The thought brought a lump to Elizabeth's throat. To be seen through Bingley's eyes, to be regarded as a gentleman ought to regard a lady, would build her confidence and make her less irritable.

Yes, Longbourn was not at all the place for her.

While Kitty unpacked her things in a bedroom upstairs, Mrs. Gardiner took the news of Kitty's recovery home to her husband. The Darcys were preparing to leave soon after when a knock at the front door was quickly followed by a voice calling, "Jane! Jane, are you home?"

Jane rushed into the foyer. "Lydia, I have told you, you are welcome here at any time, but you must be let in like any other guest." She led her towards the drawing room.

"Lord, I forgot. Indeed, it is too cold outside to wait. And what did you think of the great joke Kitty and I played? My mother will be so diverted when we all show up at Longbourn for Christmas dinner."

"And how do you expect to get to Longbourn?" Elizabeth asked, kissing her sister in greeting.

"Why, I shall ride with Kitty, of course. We will take the express, and hire a man to accompany us, and my father will pay for it when we get there."

"I think not," Darcy said. "If Kitty is to go to Longbourn, Bingley or I shall take her. Should you not spend Christmas with your husband, since he is to go back to his regiment soon?"

"Back to the north, where Colonel Fitzwilliam will try again to kill him, and leave me a widow. With Wickham only an ensign, his pension would not be near enough for me to live on."

"I shall speak to my cousin, then, and request he wait until your husband is a captain to kill him."

Lydia stared, then laughed. "Why, Darcy, I had no idea you could be funny. You're always so stiff and proper. A *proper* gentleman is no fun at all, although a *stiff* one has his uses."

"Lydia!" Elizabeth scolded.

"We are all married ladies here, Lizzy, and sisters besides. Why may I not have some fun?"

"Georgiana is not a married lady," Elizabeth said through her teeth.

"Oh, Miss Darcy, I did not notice you there in the corner. How silly of me. What a fine muslin you are wearing! You must tell me who your dressmaker is."

Elizabeth looked over to Jane, who looked frankly exhausted. Caroline Bingley might be home at any moment, and her condescending comments when she arrived to find the two youngest Bennet girls there would be enough to try even Jane's patience.

"Lydia, why don't you come to supper with Darcy and me? I've barely seen you since we've come to town."

"You want *me* to come to supper? And Darcy will not mind?"

"My quarrel with your husband does not extend to you, Lydia," Darcy said. "You are welcome in my home as often as my wife wishes."

"And perhaps we can play whist after?" Lydia asked.

"Perhaps," Elizabeth said.

"Oh, we will have such fun! I quite long to get to know Miss Darcy better."

And so it was settled to everyone's satisfaction. When Kitty came downstairs, the Darcys and Lydia said their goodbyes with hugs and tears.

⁓✻⁓

After supper, the Darcys retreated to a game of whist in the drawing room. Lydia was in a jolly mood, and raised the spirits of the others. Elizabeth had never seen Georgiana smile so much. Elizabeth could not imagine ever leaving Georgiana alone in Lydia's company, but the good humour of the youngest Bennet sister did wonders for drawing out the shy Miss Darcy.

As the evening wound down, Elizabeth said to Lydia, "Is your husband expecting you home tonight?"

"Lord, no. I told him I was going to Longbourn for Christmas, and he seemed perfectly happy to let me go."

Elizabeth fought to keep her composure. "Then you must spend the night here. I shall have a room made up for you."

"Thank you." Lydia looked at her earnestly, a rare expression on that usually laughing face. "I don't know what I would do without the kindness you and Darcy have shown me."

Elizabeth reached over and squeezed her hand.

Once a fire was lit in Lydia's bedroom and had chased away the chill, Elizabeth helped her settle in. As Elizabeth went to go, Lydia grabbed her arm. "Please, Lizzy. You must help me get to Longbourn. I need my mother." She burst into tears.

Elizabeth sat on the bed beside her and cradled her in her arms. "Dear Lydia! What is the matter?"

"Nothing is as it ought to be. Before I married him, Wickham was always in good spirits. But now he is irritable and cross. And since I gave him the best possible news, instead of being happy, he is even more put out with me."

The best possible news! Elizabeth did not dare guess what Lydia meant, though she had her suspicions. "What news?"

Lydia's lip quivered. "I am expecting a child." She wiped away her tears, but more soon followed. "All Wickham has done since I told him is to complain of another mouth to feed. He says I should have been more careful. As if *he* were not there. As if *he* could not have been more careful."

Elizabeth held her while she sobbed. A child! She felt a quick pang of jealousy, followed by overwhelming love. Though Wickham might be the father, this child would be a blessing to their family. "You mustn't despair. Jane and I will help you. With whatever you need...whatever this child needs."

"You're so kind to me, dear Lizzy, but you have never had a child. I need my mother desperately. I know my parents are unhappy that I eloped with Wickham as I did, but I never expected them to cast me out."

Until that moment, Elizabeth had never realised how ignorant Lydia truly was of how close she had come to ruining her life. Lydia had no more idea than Kitty of how despicable Wickham's actions were, or how unguarded were her own. She still seemed to believe that Wickham had intended to marry her all along.

Elizabeth was grateful beyond words that the disaster had been averted. She stroked her sister's hair fondly. "No one has cast you out. Jane says our mother talks of you constantly. She misses you beyond measure. After Wickham goes back to his regiment, I am sure you will be welcome at Longbourn."

"If only you could see the rooms where we are staying. They are small and cramped and dark. I was so eager to come to London, but all I have seen of it so far is that hovel. I long to go to the theatre, but I don't even have any decent clothes."

"What of the wedding clothes my parents bought?"

"I cannot afford a laundress."

"Oh, Lydia. Tomorrow we will get your clothes and have them laundered. And then we will find a decent place for you to stay until the new year, when Wickham goes to the north and you go to Longbourn."

"Do you really believe my father might let me visit?"

"I think my father misses you dreadfully, though he would never admit it."

"You don't know what a weight this lifts off of me. I have no idea how to raise a child. Wickham will be with his regiment, and I shall be all alone."

"You will never be alone. I promise you that."

"Do you think...Darcy might consent to be my child's godfather?"

Elizabeth considered a moment. "Perhaps you had better ask Bingley."

Lydia nodded. "Can you tell me why Darcy hates Wickham so? Is it because Wickham tried to elope with Miss Darcy?"

Elizabeth stared, shock and horror warring in her breast. "Wickham told you about that?"

Lydia shook her head. "I put it together. And I thought, if he once loved Miss Darcy, then if I studied her and acted more like her, perhaps he would love me again, too."

The desolation in Lydia's voice broke Elizabeth's heart. "He was never in love with Miss Darcy. Perhaps he cared for her, as he had known her all her life. But it was her thirty thousand pounds he wanted, not Miss Darcy. I can only think that since you did not have thirty thousand pounds, that he must have liked you for yourself."

A faint smile touched Lydia's lips. "Sometimes, when he is not in a foul mood, he says that he is irritable because of his injury. It was quite painful at first, and he could barely walk. I was a terrible nursemaid and could not help him. I am not fit to be a wife!"

"You were never taught any of those things. You've never cared for an infant or an invalid—you are unprepared, not unfit. My mother can help you. Jane can help you. And perhaps you can come to Pemberley for a time to be closer to Wickham when he is back with his regiment. You are not alone in this world. You have your family. And I am sorry indeed that you ever thought otherwise."

Chapter 4

When Jane visited the next morning, Elizabeth passed on Lydia's news. Jane shook her head at Wickham's response. "He cannot truly be unhappy that Lydia is having a child?"

"I cannot pretend to understand the workings of the mind of George Wickham. But if I had to guess, I would say that he's frightened of being responsible for another person when he can barely be responsible for himself. Think about it, Jane. He was raised in one of the greatest houses of Derbyshire as if he were part of the family—but he was not part of the family. Once he reached his majority, he was sent out to make his way in the world. Something he was ill-prepared for, if not by education, then by temperament. Since that time, he's made a series of terrible decisions that have cost him his friends and his reputation. Is such a man prepared to be a father?"

"Lydia's children will want for nothing. He must know that."

"I would love to know what he has done with the money Darcy settled on Lydia when Wickham married her. He is certainly not spending it on Lydia. The interest on it should be enough for them to live comfortably, if not extravagantly. If he has gambled it away, Lydia is better off moving back to Longbourn permanently."

"Surely that cannot be the case!"

"Perhaps he is simply economising. Or perhaps he'd rather spend it on himself than on his wife."

Jane smoothed her skirt. "Would it be best to find out?"

Elizabeth smiled. "You mean, have Darcy talk to him."

"The other option would be Colonel Fitzwilliam."

"Since he is clearly frightened of Colonel Fitzwilliam, that might be a better choice."

"Perhaps." Jane sighed. "Can you imagine the three of them playing as boys together, and now it has come to this?"

Outside the window, icicles clinging to the eaves glistened in the sun, water dripping from their tips. "Perhaps there is some plan in this. Their children will be cousins, God willing. They will not be able to avoid one another completely. Perhaps in time..."

Elizabeth shook her head, then continued, "I was wrong yesterday, to say Wickham is capable of violence against Kitty. I have no proof that he is vicious. I shall cherish in my heart the hope that he will become a better man, that fatherhood perhaps can change him. I shall not count on it, but I shall hope."

At the sound of horses, Elizabeth looked outside through the window of her front parlour. She thought for a moment that her eyes deceived her, but however many times she blinked, they were still there—her father, mother, and sister Mary stepping out of a carriage, servants unloading the trunks.

Elizabeth wanted to be cross, but she missed her family and was thrilled to find them suddenly deposited at her front door. She threw on her shawl and went out to greet them.

"What do you think, my dear?" her father asked. "If my daughters will not come to Longbourn, then Longbourn must come to my daughters."

"Come here, Mrs. Darcy," her mother said. "I must look at you. Oh, you are indeed every bit the lady I thought you would be! That dress is the finest weave I have ever seen. As I told Mr. Bennet, I *shall* have all my daughters with me at Christmas. This is quite an inconvenience to the Gardiners, I am sure, but they will have to have Christmas at home this year. My sister Philips was quite cross when I told her of our change in plans, but it could not be helped. Kitty!" she called as she headed inside the house. "Where is my Kitty!"

"I have never seen such nonsense in my life," Mary said as she and Elizabeth each took one of their father's arms and walked towards the front door. "My mother never has a kind word for Kitty, but when Kitty disappears for a day and a half, it is as if my mother were torn to pieces. Perhaps I should disappear, too. I could hide in Netherfield cottage for a day. With a fire in the fireplace, and a basket of fruit and cheese, I could be quite comfortable."

"Perhaps I could hide with you," her father said.

As they stepped inside and Mary took off her bonnet, Elizabeth said in her father's ear, "I have news, Papa, and this time, you cannot hide from it."

"That sounds very grave indeed."

"Not grave. Serious." She led him into the study and closed the door. "Kitty came to London as part of a scheme Lydia hatched so she could go to Longbourn for Christmas. It was not a sensible scheme, but she is desperate. Papa, Lydia is having a child, and she needs to be with her mother."

He stared a long moment before recovering himself. "A child! Well, I should not be surprised, she has been married these four months. I can comprehend how the dear girl would want to be close to her mother. And what does Wickham think of all this?"

"I am of the impression that Wickham does not care one way or another *what* Lydia does."

"So soon! I would have wagered it would be at least a twelve-month before he thoroughly tired of her. But then, Lydia is an excessively silly girl."

"Papa, you must not say such things. Lydia may be selfish and headstrong and cunning—but she loves you, and she values your good opinion. Kitty, too. If all they hear from you is how silly they are, how can you expect them to become anything else? Lydia will soon be a mother, and she is terrified. She does not believe she is capable of it. You can help convince her that she is. You must. It is your duty."

Mr. Bennet nodded thoughtfully. "You're right, my girl. I cannot give this child a good father, but I can give it a good grandfather. You can count on me, my dear."

She gave him a smile and a nod, but the heaviness in her heart would not dissipate. Yes, she could count on her father, and so could Jane. He had lavished them with praise all their lives. But he had been a very different sort of father to her younger sisters—

especially Lydia and Kitty, who took after their mother.

He had married his wife for her beauty and vivacious nature, and discovered too late that the difference in their intellects and temperaments made them ill-suited as mates. His greatest pleasure in life was in vexing her, which was fortunate for him, as she was easily vexed. He paid no more care to soothing the tempers of his daughters than he did of his wife. Indeed, the only person's comfort he seemed to care for was his own. As long as he was sequestered in his library, away from the noise of the females of the household, he was happy.

Elizabeth loved her father dearly, and hated to think ill of him even for a moment. She would put her anger to good use, to ensure the well-being of her sisters. The role seemed to fall to her and Jane, and she was not sorry for it.

How Darcy would react was a different matter.

That night, Elizabeth was reading in bed when Darcy joined her. Her parents were sleeping in a guest room, and Mary at the Bingleys'.

Lydia had been in raptures at the reunion with her mother. Happy tears soon gave way to laughter and hours of ceaseless conversation, until the two had quite exhausted themselves. Though both were of a stout constitution, Lydia's delicate condition depleted her energy, and Mrs. Bennet's nerves were ever in want of a rest.

Mr. Bennet had given Kitty a good scolding, but her contrite tears softened his heart. When she promised never to disobey him in such a shocking manner again, he embraced her and said she was a good girl. He readily gave his permission for her to stay in town with the Gardiners for the season, especially once it was decided that Lydia would go to Longbourn for a time after Wickham returned to his regiment—therefore reducing the likelihood of any further conspiracies between them.

Elizabeth and Jane were both satisfied with this outcome. They would not be unhappy for the company of their younger sisters, when taken one at a time. Still, Elizabeth could not help feeling she was imposing on Darcy.

"You will not be sorry to have Kitty join us at Pemberley in the spring?"

"Not at all. She will be a good companion for Georgiana."

"They will be good for each other."

Darcy drew her into his arms. "You must stop apologising to me for your family. After the abominable way Lady Catherine has treated you, I can hardly claim that my relations hold the advantage when it comes to civility. At least your sisters have youth and inexperience as a defence."

"I hold out hope that they will grow into sensible women by the time they are five-and-thirty."

"Perhaps even by five-and-twenty," he teased.

She stroked his cheek, enjoying the rough feel of a day's growth of whiskers. "Sometimes I worry that this happiness cannot last—that somehow it is an illusion, and you will soon lose patience with me."

"I went into this marriage with my eyes open, as did you. We have both of us seen the worst of the other and our relations. I cannot imagine two people better suited for happiness in marriage than we are." He kissed her hand. "Perhaps I had better remind you of how dear you are to me, Elizabeth."

"Perhaps you had better." She arched her brows, and he buried his face in her neck, covering her with kisses.

Chapter 5

On the twenty-fifth, after a day of visiting and merrymaking, Darcy and Elizabeth arrived at the Bingleys' in the early evening. Despite being introduced to some of the more illustrious of Darcy's acquaintance, including two members of the House of Lords, Elizabeth felt secure in having acquitted herself well. Darcy had been all smiles in response to the congratulations he received on his marriage, looking at her with pure delight in his eyes. She could not help but be gratified.

She entered Jane's town house dressed in red velvet, a ruby-studded cross at her throat. Darcy's hand was warm on her arm as the butler led them into the drawing room.

Her entire family was there assembled, including Mr. and Mrs. Gardiner. Jane greeted her with a kiss.

"Oh Lizzy, is it not wonderful. Mama was right. There is nothing like having all of one's family together at Christmas."

Caroline Bingley was there too, speaking in whispers to her sister, Mrs. Hurst. Elizabeth did not speculate on what remarks Miss Bingley might be making about her new in-laws. Elizabeth was prepared to think graciously of everyone on this one day a year.

This included her brother Wickham, whom she was surprised to see at his wife's side. He smiled at Elizabeth pleasantly, and even gave a slight bow in Darcy's direction, which Darcy deigned to return. Elizabeth patted her husband's arm, and he kissed her temple tenderly.

Lydia came over to her and said in low tones, "Can you believe it? Wickham apologised most profusely for being out of temper when Kitty came to visit. He has even started teasing me about names for the baby. He says if it is a boy, we must call him Denny. He knows Mr. Denny was in love with me, and is determined to vex me for it."

Her expression clouded, and she turned to Mary at the pianoforte. "Must you play something so sombre on Christmas? Give us a jig instead. I long to dance!"

Some furniture was moved, and while Wickham stood up with Lydia, Bingley danced with Kitty. Amidst the noise, a new visitor joined them.

"Darcy," said Colonel Fitzwilliam clapping his back, "I must have just missed you at my father's. Lady Adelaide said I could find you here. It was wise of you to leave Georgiana in her company, while there was a chance of *that* gentleman being here."

He nodded towards Wickham, who caught sight of him and paled. He recovered himself the next moment and gave a deep bow.

"Wickham my man," Colonel Fitzwilliam said, "good to see that leg of yours has healed! You must be quite well to dance so vigorously."

"My recovery is nearly complete, sir, as the surgeon assured you it would be."

"Glad to hear it. I look forward to your return to the north."

"As do I, sir, for there is nothing I loathe so much as idleness. I shall be quite happy to make myself useful again."

Elizabeth looked at her husband slyly, a glance he returned.

While Darcy and his cousin engaged in conversation, Elizabeth paid her respects to the Gardiners. As they had other visits to make, she accompanied them out as they took their leave. On her way back to the drawing room, she happened to overhear an exchange between Colonel Fitzwilliam and Mr. Wickham.

"I hope there has not been some problem with your pay reaching you?" the colonel asked. "I had a hint from your lovely wife that your rooms here in London are not in the style to which she is accustomed."

"The fault is all mine, sir," Wickham conceded. "I rented rooms of a sort that suited me as a bachelor. I failed to consider that while a soldier may be content sleeping in an open field, his wife may require more felicitous accommodations."

"Quite right." Colonel Fitzwilliam winked at him. "I imagine you will not forget again, eh, old boy?"

"No, sir, I shall not." Wickham laughed.

"Capital." Colonel Fitzwilliam patted his back. "One more thing, old friend. While we have had our differences in the past, I assure you that as your commanding officer, I bear you no ill will. If I had indeed tried to kill you," the colonel said pointedly, "I should not have failed."

Colonel Fitzwilliam bowed and sauntered off, leaving Wickham pale and wide-eyed.

Elizabeth walked up to Wickham and took his arm. "How fortunate that your regiment removed from Newcastle. With you stationed within easy distance of Derbyshire, perhaps I can attend on Lydia during her confinement."

"She...yes, that would be quite good of you."

"You are fortunate in your commanding officer. Colonel Fitzwilliam is a man of some influence, with his father in the House of Lords. The colonel's being a childhood friend of yours may make him more tolerant than another man might be. Yet even his patience has an end. He is not a man to look kindly on one who spends his pay on drink and gambling, rather than on his wife and child."

"No, of course not. He is every bit the gentleman."

She patted his arm. "I am happy, brother, to see that you and I are of one mind on this."

"Indeed, dear Elizabeth. I value your friendship as always."

"You can trust that Lydia's well-being is of the greatest consequence to me."

He gave her a nod. "I appreciate all your kind attentions to my wife."

"She is never far from my thoughts, as I am sure she is never far from yours."

With a bow, he went back to Lydia, who had apparently tired of dancing and sat by the fire.

Darcy came and took Elizabeth's arm. "May I ask what that was about?"

"I was reminding my brother Wickham that Lydia is not the inconsequential girl he thought he was marrying. She is allied to a powerful family now, who expect him to do right by her."

"I suspect he will need continual reminders of that nature."

"As may be. I shall not let him forget."

He cradled her hand in his. "You seem to be taking well to your new-found power, madam."

"I shall do my best to use it for good rather than evil."

"I hope you will not be good *all* the time." He kissed her gloved palm discreetly.

"On our trips to the Cotswolds, I shall be as naughty as can be."

He drew his brow. "I do not apprehend you, madam."

"It is a joke between Jane and me." She caught her sister's eye, Jane holding her own husband's arm, looking like an angel in a white gown with gold trim, her blond hair glistening in the candlelight. A contented smile graced her lips, one Elizabeth mimicked. They both had found true happiness, and the means to share it with others. And that was the greatest felicity one could hope for in life.

The End

About the Author

Andrea David is a Regency romance author in Raleigh, North Carolina. When she's not reading or writing, she enjoys gardening, scuba diving, and hiking active volcanoes with her husband. To learn more about her books, visit her website at AndreaDavidAuthor.com.

More Books by Andrea David

Darcy Comes to Rosings

Elizabeth Bennet from Jane Austen's *Pride and Prejudice* is enjoying a visit with her newly married best friend in the idyllic countryside of Kent. Her pleasant holiday is interrupted when the arrogant Mr. Darcy appears at nearby Rosings Park. During their frequent meetings, her spirited retorts do nothing to deter his attentions to her. In fact, they only seem to encourage him.

Realizing Darcy is in love with her, Elizabeth is torn by an awful dilemma. With her father's estate entailed on a male heir, she and her sisters face the prospect of poverty if they do not marry well. Darcy's wealth could save them. But how can she marry a man she does not esteem simply for the material comfort he can offer?

Fitzwilliam Darcy is determined to forget the lovely Elizabeth, who stole his heart during his autumn sojourn in Hertfordshire. So naturally, when he learns she is spending the spring within walking distance of his aunt's estate at Rosings, he goes for an extended stay. He finds Elizabeth even more enchanting than he remembered.

When Darcy discovers Elizabeth's rightful resentments against him, he seeks to make things right and court her properly. Can he convince her of his worth? Or have his past sins—and the machinations of an old enemy—sunk him in her opinion forever?

This sweet Regency romance is a full-length, standalone novel. It includes kissing and a fade-to-black wedding night scene.

Made in the USA
Middletown, DE
05 April 2023

28294738R00056